CAN'T SLEEP

Chris Raschka

SCHOLASTIC INC.
New York Toronto London Auckland Sydney

Poone

ISBN 0-590-29546-2

Copyright © 1995 by Christopher Raschka.
All rights reserved. Published by Scholastic Inc., 555 Broadway, New York, NY 10012, by arrangement with
Orchard Books.

12 11 10 9 8 7 6 5 4 3 2 1   7 8 9/9 0 1 2/0

Printed in the U.S.A.   08

First Scholastic printing, January 1997

The text of this book is set in 24 point Korinna.

The illustrations are watercolor paintings reproduced in full color.

For Paul and Renate

When you can't sleep
the moon will keep

you safe. The moon
will stay awake.

When your big brother
goes to bed

and sleeps
and you can't sleep,

the moon will watch
you in your room.

When you can't sleep   your mother moving
and you now hear   in the hall,

in the bathroom
washing up, and

closing her door

the moon will rise
and see you in

your bed and see
your open eyes.

When you can't sleep
when you now hear

your father turning
off the lights

and walking down
the hall and shutting
that door tight,

the moon will hear,
the moon will hear
this too.

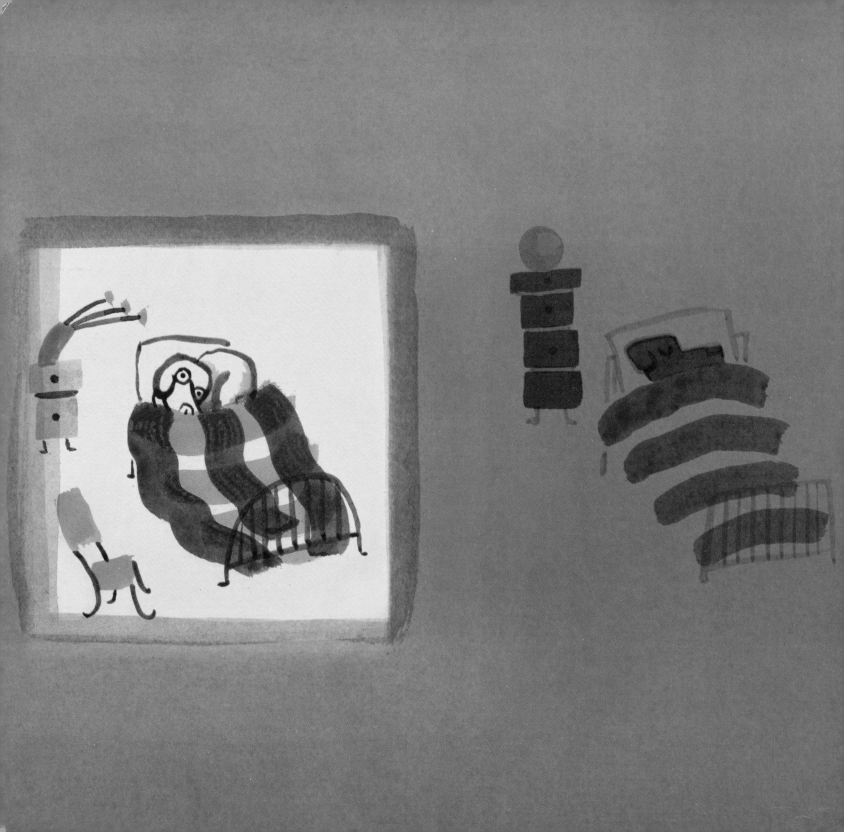

Now when there is
no sound

the moon can tell
you feel frightened
and are lonely.

The moon will stay
awake for you.

The moon will stay
awake for you
until you too
are sleeping.

When morning comes

the moon will go

to bed. Now you   may stay awake

and keep her safe . . .

you'll keep her safe.